(4)

BWB

E
W

Wolff, Ashley.

A year of birds

842202

DATE DUE

OCT 1 9 1985		

A Year of Birds

A Year of Birds

Ashley Wolff

Dodd, Mead & Company • New York

Copyright © 1984 by Ashley Wolff
All rights reserved • No part of this book may be reproduced in any form
without permission in writing from the publisher • Distributed in Canada
by McClelland and Stewart Limited, Toronto
Printed in Hong Kong by South China Printing Company
1 2 3 4 5 6 7 8 9 10

Library of Congress Cataloging in Publication Data

Wolff, Ashley.
  A year of birds.

  Summary: Labeled pictures disclose the many kinds
of birds that visit a child's home during each month
of the year.
  1. Birds—Juvenile literature. 2. Seasons—
Juvenile literature. [1. Birds—Pictorial works.
2. Months—Pictorial works] I. Title.
QL676.2.W65 1984   598   83-27470
ISBN 0-396-08313-7

For my parents,
Dean and Klaus

In winter, in spring,
in summer, and in fall—
in every month of the year
all kinds of birds
visit Ellie's house.

Grosbeaks, purple finches, and

black-capped chickadees in January

Cardinals and a sparrow

in February

Canada geese and a robin

in March

Robins and a warbler in April

Redwing blackbirds in May

A bluebird, a goldfinch, wrens,

and baby robins in June

Ruby-throated hummingbirds

in July

Mallard ducks in August

Partridges and ring-necked

pheasants in September

Canada geese in October

Juncos, a nuthatch, a woodpecker,

a cardinal, and a finch in November

A dove, a bluejay, a titmouse, and

other winter birds in December.